BUNNY BUSINESS

by NANCY POYDAR

Holiday House / New York

Library of Congress Cataloging-in-Publication Data
Poydar, Nancy.
Bunny business / Nancy Poydar.—1st ed.
        p.   cm.
Summary: When his class performs a spring play about rabbits,
Harry proves that he is a good listener after all.
ISBN 0-8234-1771-9
[1. Theater—Fiction. 2. Schools—Fiction.
3. Listening—Fiction. 4. Behavior—Fiction.
5. Rabbits—Fiction.] I. Title.
PZ7.P8846 Bu 2003
[E]—dc21   2002068573

For Ali Rafiy, forever young

Once on a spring day, Harry spotted a puddle under the swings. "Mud!" He nudged George.

"Harry," called Ms. Finch. "We're talking about spring and you're not listening."

Harry was better at jumping in mud than listening.

Ms. Finch was so excited
her bird earrings were flying.
"Who would like to be in a spring
play about bunnies?" she asked.
Everyone's hand flew up.

Harry waved his hand too, but he wasn't sure he would be good at being in a play.

"I'll read the story," said Ms. Finch. "You think about which bunny you want to be."

"*Bunny Business,*" she read. "*Once, on a spring day. . .*" Ms. Finch droned on.

A fly! Harry poked Chandelle and *buzz, buzzed.*
"*Shhh!*" said Chandelle.
"Harry!" scolded Ms. Finch. "It's listening time."
Harry was better at *buzz, buzzing* like a fly than listening.

Finally, Ms. Finch finished reading. "*And so, it was clear to all the creatures of Bunny Hollow that it wasn't just the flowers that bloomed on that magic spring day. The End.*"

"I want to be
Uncle Cabbage,"
said George at
recess. "He's the star.
Amy and Simon want
to be Honey Bunny
and Sunny Bunny.
Which bunny do
you want to be,
Harry?"

Harry wished he had
listened. He'd have to
think of something to
say to Ms. Finch when
she asked him.

The next day Ms. Finch said they should listen like bunnies. "Time to make our bunny ears," she chirped.

Harry pretended to have sonar! *"Ping, ping."*

Harry was better at pretending than listening. He missed the directions. *"Ping, ping, ping."*

Harry
asked
Chandelle
what to do.
Chandelle
was busy.

Harry asked
Amy what to do.
Amy was busy.

I'll do it my own way! Harry thought.
Harry was good at figuring things out.

When he finished, Harry's bunny ears were
different.
They drooped like thirsty plants.
Everyone snickered.
Amy pointed. "Too big!"

"Too big is BETTER!" declared Harry.
"Better at what?" asked George.
Harry knew what the answer had to be.

"Listening," he said.
"Are you sure?" asked Ms. Finch.
Harry would make sure. He nodded.
Flip, flop went his big ears. Flip, flop.

Ms. Finch's bunnies
rehearsed every day. When
they practiced the Bunny Song,
Funny Bunny listened and sang.
When they did the Bunny Dance,
Funny Bunny listened and danced.

They all learned their parts by heart, except for Harry. Harry got so good at listening that he learned *everyone's* part. Ms. Finch had to put her finger in front of her lips when it *wasn't* his turn to speak.

At last, their spring play was ready. Everyone came. The bunnies took their places. Uncle Cabbage opened his mouth to begin.

Nothing came out! The audience gasped.

Funny Bunny hopped forward. Everyone laughed.
Harry was good at making people laugh.
"*Welcome to Bunny Business,*" he began.
Ms. Finch did not put her finger over her lips.
Funny Bunny continued pretending the words
were his. "*Once, on a spring day...*"

Harry stopped speaking when Uncle Cabbage finally found his voice. Ms. Finch didn't need to remind him because everyone could see that Harry was better at starring in spring plays than spoiling them.

At last, Uncle Cabbage said, "*And so, it was clear to all the creatures of Bunny Hollow that it wasn't just the flowers that bloomed on that magic spring day. The End.*"

All the bunnies bowed. The audience clapped
for each bunny, but they clapped the loudest
for Funny Bunny.

It was so loud, Harry had to cover his ears.
The End

Time to Make Bunny Ears

You will need scissors, a stapler, heavy paper, and crayons or markers.

1. Cut a strip of paper about 2 inches wide that is long enough to fit around your head.

2. Staple it together in a band that will fit around your head.

3. Fold a piece of 8 $\frac{1}{2}$-by-11-inch paper in half the long way.

4. Draw a bunny ear about 2 inches wide and 8 inches long, making it slightly wider and rounded at the top.

5. Cut the paper while it is folded to get two bunny ears.

6. Color the insides pink or red.

7. Staple the ears onto your paper headband.

8. Now, listen like a bunny!

Can you make bunny ears like Harry's?